Ju
F
C26   Caseley, Judith.
          When Grandpa came to
       stay.

When Grandpa Came to Stay

by JUDITH CASELEY

GREENWILLOW BOOKS, New York

The three-color preseparated art was prepared as
pen-and-ink line with the three overlays done in gray tones.
The text type is Bembo. The display type is Serif Gothic Outline.

Printed in the United States of America   First Edition
1 2 3 4 5 6 7 8 9 10

Library of Congress Cataloging in Publication Data

Caseley, Judith.   When Grandpa came to stay.
Summary: When Grandpa comes to his house to stay, Benny
enjoys his company and helps him cope with Grandma's death.
[1. Grandfathers—Fiction. 2. Jews—Fiction. 3. Death—Fiction]
I. Title.   PZ7.C2677Wh 1986   [E]   85-12616
ISBN 0-688-06128-1   ISBN 0-688-06129-X (lib. bdg.)

To Susan and Libby
and Ava, with love

One snowy Sunday, Benny was out in the yard
building a snowman. Mrs. Gold was clearing the
sidewalk. A car pulled up, and in the front seat
was an old man.

He lifted one leg out and then the other. He held
a cane with a bird on the end of it.

"Grandpa!" cried Benny.

"Papa!" cried Mrs. Gold. "You've finally arrived."

It was Grandpa's first visit since Grandma had died.
Mrs. Gold took his suitcase, and Mr. Gold helped
Grandpa up the steep driveway.

It was lunchtime, and Mrs. Gold served Grandpa a
bowl of soup.
"Borscht!" cried Grandpa to Benny. "My favorite soup!"
Then he spooned some thick sour cream into the bowl.
"While Grandpa is visiting," said Mrs. Gold, "he gets
his borscht every day."
"When I was a boy," said Grandpa, "my father used to
sing me a song.

> *Ei yi yi boychik. Ei yi yi boychik.*
> *Ei yi boychik loves his borscht.*
> *He loves it in the winter.*
> *He loves it in the summer.*
> *Ei yi yi yi boychik loves his borscht."*

Mr. Gold told Grandpa to make himself at home.
So, Grandpa put the pillow that Grandma had knitted
on his bed. He unpacked his shaving brush and his
favorite mug.
Benny put it next to his favorite cup with ducks on it.
Grandpa put a picture of Grandma on the dresser.
"When Grandma was a girl," he told Benny, "her hair
was the same color as yours."
"And Mommy says I have your eyes," said Benny.
"So you do," Grandpa said.

Every day Benny put a black ball in Grandpa's hand for exercise. Grandpa pressed his fingers around it. Benny set the timer for fifteen minutes, and when the bell rang he yelled, "Time!" Then Grandpa would stop.

Every night Grandpa dressed for dinner in a suit
and bow tie.
"When I look good, I feel good," he said.
Benny helped Grandpa put on his socks and tie his
shoelaces. Benny put on a bow tie, too.
Step by step, down the stairs Grandpa went, holding
on to the railing.
Benny waited at the bottom and gave Grandpa his
cane. Then they went in to dinner.
Every meal Mrs. Gold cut up Grandpa's food and
Mr. Gold gave him his borscht.
"Ei yi yi boychik," sang Benny.
"Ei yi yi boychik loves his borscht," sang Grandpa.

After dinner, Mrs. Gold washed the dishes and
Grandpa dried. He was very slow.
"Boychik," said Grandpa. "When I'm done, we'll
all play cards."
Benny held the cards for Grandpa and they were
partners.
Grandpa laughed when they lost. Then he and
Benny had milk and cookies.
"To cheer us up!" said Benny.

One evening, suddenly, Grandpa started to cry.
"I miss your mother," he said to Mrs. Gold.
"I miss your grandma," he said to Benny.
Grandpa covered his face with his hands.
Benny looked at Grandpa. He looked at his
mother and father.
"I don't like grandpas that cry!" he shouted.
And Benny ran to his room.

Mrs. Gold followed him.

"Sometimes," she said, "grown-ups are sad.
Sometimes grandpas cry. And sometimes mothers
and fathers cry, too."

"Are you sad, Mommy?" asked Benny.

"I'm very sad," said Mrs. Gold, "because I miss
Grandma, too."

Benny heard Grandpa coming up the stairs. Grandpa knocked on the door.

"May I come in?" he asked.

"No," said Benny.

Grandpa opened the door.

Benny looked down. "I was mean," he said.

"I was no angel when I was a boy," said Grandpa.

"You weren't?" said Benny.

"No," said Grandpa, "and I'm still no angel. I got mad at your grandma lots of times."

"And were you friends again?" asked Benny.

"Of course," said Grandpa. "Just like you and I are friends."

He hugged Benny.

The next day, Grandpa said to Benny, "You and I are going on a trip. Just the two of us."
Grandpa packed a bag and put on his overcoat with a flower in the buttonhole. Then he put on his finest hat.
"A fedora," he said, "the best hat in the world."
"A Yankee cap," said Benny, "the best team in the world."

They walked to the bus stop and waited. The snow had melted and the birds were singing.

"It feels like spring," cried Grandpa.

"Here comes our bus," cried Benny.

The bus pulled up and Grandpa climbed the steps slowly.

"He was sick," Benny said to the bus driver, "but he's better now."

They looked out the window together.

"This is our stop," said Grandpa.
There were lots of trees, and Grandpa showed Benny
some daffodils.
"We take this little path here," said Grandpa.
"Isn't this a pretty place? Your Grandma is here."
"But Grandma is dead," said Benny.
"That's right," said Grandpa. "This is her resting place."
Grandpa took Benny's hand. "Let's find Grandma,"
he said.

They walked down the path. Flowers were everywhere.
Benny read the names.
"Sarah Levy," he said to Grandpa. "My grandma."
Grandpa and Benny sat quietly on a bench.
Then Grandpa took out a thermos and gave Benny a
cup and some cookies.
"We'll drink tea with Grandma," he said. "Grandma
loved cookies, too."

Grandpa took a potted plant out of his bag.
"These are tulips, tulips for Grandma," he said.
They dug a hole and placed the tulips in the ground.
Benny watered the flowers and Grandpa said a
blessing. And then they went home.

In the kitchen, Mrs. Gold gave them big bowls of soup.
"I planted flowers," said Benny. "And I said hello to Grandma."
"Ei yi yi boychik," said Grandpa.
And they ate their borscht.

Temple Israel

Minneapolis, Minnesota

```
        IN MEMORY OF
        KAY GALINSON
           FROM
     JOANNE KRUIDENIER
```